# Tricky Tricks

# Tricky Tricks

Written and illustrated by
**Sally Kindberg**

LUTTERWORTH PRESS
Cambridge

## FOR EMERALD

**Lutterworth Press
7 All Saints' Passage
Cambridge CB2 3LS**

*British Library Cataloguing in Publication Data*

Kindberg, Sally
  Tricky tricks.
  1. Tricks — Juvenile literature
  I. Title
  793.8    GV1548

ISBN 0-7188-2654-X

Copyright © Sally Kindberg 1986
First published 1986

All rights reserved. No part of this publication may
be reproduced, stored in a retrieval system, or
transmitted in any form or by any means, electronic,
mechanical, photocopying, recording, or otherwise,
without the prior permission in writing of the publisher.

Printed in Singapore

# CONTENTS

## CONFUSE YOUR FRIENDS

| | |
|---|---|
| Floating Shrunken Head | 1 |
| Vanishing Flower | 4 |
| The Mummified Finger | 6 |
| Visit from Outer Space | 8 |
| Rubbery Egg | 10 |
| Disappearing Handkerchief | 12 |
| Funny Loops | 15 |
| Horrid Hunger | 18 |
| Card in the Hat | 20 |

## TYING PEOPLE UP

| | |
|---|---|
| Tied Up in a Sack | 22 |
| Tangle Torture | 26 |

## STRONG PEOPLE DEFEATED

| | |
|---|---|
| Immobilize a Bossy Person | 32 |
| Stuck to the Floor | 33 |
| Five Bricks with One Hand | 34 |

## SECRET MESSAGES

| | |
|---|---|
| Telepathic Tips | 36 |
| Blank Pages | 42 |

## FUN IN THE DARK

| | |
|---|---|
| Gruesome Duck | 46 |
| Giant Spider | 47 |
| Baying Dog | 48 |
| Flapping Thing | 49 |
| Unexpected Goose | 50 |
| Lurking Stranger | 51 |

# CONFUSE YOUR FRIENDS
## Floating Shrunken Head

In this trick, exhibit a horrible shrunken head which appears to move from one hand to another when you rest it on a table.

You can make the grinning skull easily by cutting out a mask and sticking it to the front of an empty yoghurt pot or paper cup.

If you have more time you could build a papier-mâché head around the pot or cup and paint it in mouldy colours.

Make a hole on either side of the pot and thread black cotton through the holes.
Make a loop at A for your left thumb, and loop the cotton round your right thumb at B. The cotton is secured with tape at C just underneath the right-hand hole.

Make sure that your thumbs are in the correct loops, and that loop A is close to the left-hand hole.
Then, as you slowly pull your hands apart, the head will slide along the table in a ghastly manner.

## Vanishing Flower

Drop a small flower head (or a pompom or similar brightly coloured object) into a glass in which you have previously carefully placed a hairnet.

Then cover the glass with a handkerchief.

Remove it with a flourish and the flower has vanished!

## The Mummified Finger

Show your friends a really wonderful relic and then wiggle your finger a bit to give them a fright.

Cut out holes in the outer case and the drawer of a large matchbox and fit them together.

You could cover your finger with talc or white paint, and line the box with crumpled tissues, or other bandage-type material.

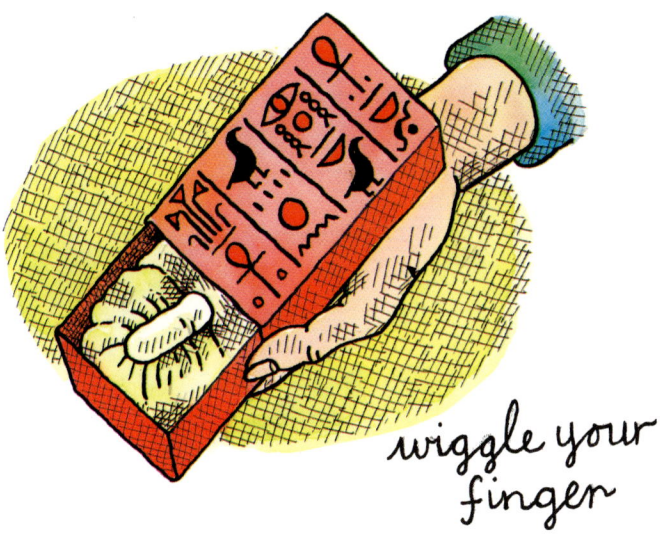

*wiggle your finger*

Insert your finger in the matchbox and startle viewers of this ancient marvel.

## Visit from Outer Space

Tell your neighbours that alien beings have visited your home and affected objects in a strange way — things have been flying through the window-panes!

Carefully saw through some everyday objects and glue the two halves on either side of the glass. Use streaks of soap to make crack marks.

You can use double-sided tape for light objects. Plastic dolls are very effective.

## Rubbery Egg

Can you bounce an egg?

Confuse your audience with a specially prepared egg, which you have soaked in strong vinegar for two days and taken out of the solution just before the demonstration.

Place your egg amongst some ordinary ones, but be careful to remember which one it is.

Take the special egg and tell the audience that by throwing the egg with superior skill it is possible to make it bounce.

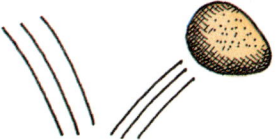

After your successful egg-bouncing, some of your friends may want to test their skill, and this could be quite messy!

## Disappearing Handkerchief

Fasten the end of a short piece of elastic to one corner of a handkerchief.

You will need to experiment with various lengths of elastic before you find one which is right for the length of your arm.
Pin the other end of the elastic inside your sleeve under the arm.

Show the handkerchief and crumple it between your hands.

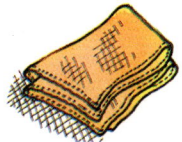

Release the handkerchief, stretching out your arms at the same time.

WHIZZ! The handkerchief has disappeared!

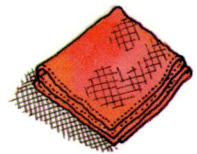

## Funny Loops

Ask a friend to cut a loop of paper in half to make two separate loops and show that this may not be very easy — the result is an even larger one, or two loops which are joined together.

Glue the ends of a very long piece of paper, making sure that the strip is twisted once before the ends are joined if you want the larger single loop.

Twist the paper twice if you want two linked loops.

Some people might get carried away trying to make it work!

## Horrid Hunger

Make your friends feel really sick by pretending to eat nasty things.

Discover some slugs in a lettuce and chew them up.

Gobble up some goldfish or bite into an apple and munch up a few worms.

Make the slithery slugs out of marzipan and paint them with diluted food dye. Be careful you don't eat a real one!

The goldfish can be made of slivers cut from a large carrot placed amongst plastic greenery in a goldfish bowl of water.

You can make convincing worms by painting bits of cooked macaroni or spaghetti with food dye and inserting them in holes made in fruit with a knitting needle.

## Card in the Hat

Ask you friends if they can drop one card at a time into an upturned hat on the floor.

They will probably not succeed because they will drop each card vertically.

Now show them how easy it is by dropping each one parallel to the ground.

# TYING PEOPLE UP
## Tied up in a Sack

Get someone to tie you up in a sack, and miraculously escape from your dark prison, leaving the sack with its original knots intact.

You will need a large sack with a long cord or string running under a hem at the mouth of it.

The hem must have an extra unstitched gap in it on the inside, so that as you climb into the sack you can secretly pull a piece of the cord down into the sack with you.

The neck of the sack is then tied up with elaborate knots.

Hop behind a screen or bush so that you are completely hidden.

Let go of the slack cord and you can easily get out.

Snip off the spare piece of cord with a pair of blunt-ended scissors which you luckily had hidden on your person.

Tie up the loose ends of the remaining cord and tuck them under the hem.

You are free, but the sack is still tied.

## Tangle Torture

Join two people with string in a very simple way and then tell them to disentangle themselves without slipping the loops from their wrists. Although at first it seems easy, it can be very frustrating. This is a good trick to play at parties — you can tangle a whole roomful of people.

After they have tangled themselves into a temper, show them how it is done.

# Tangle Torture

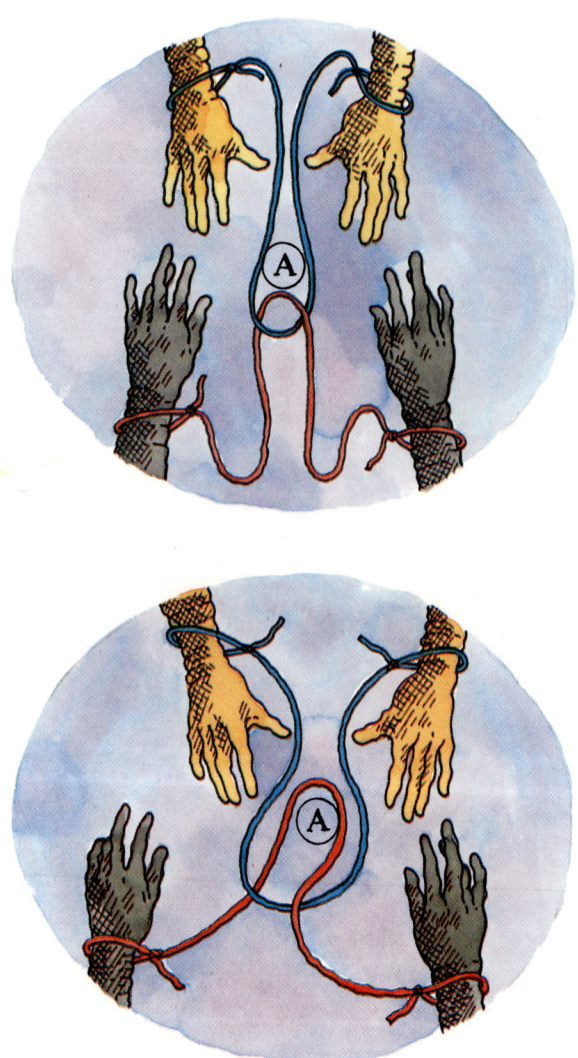

# Tangle Torture

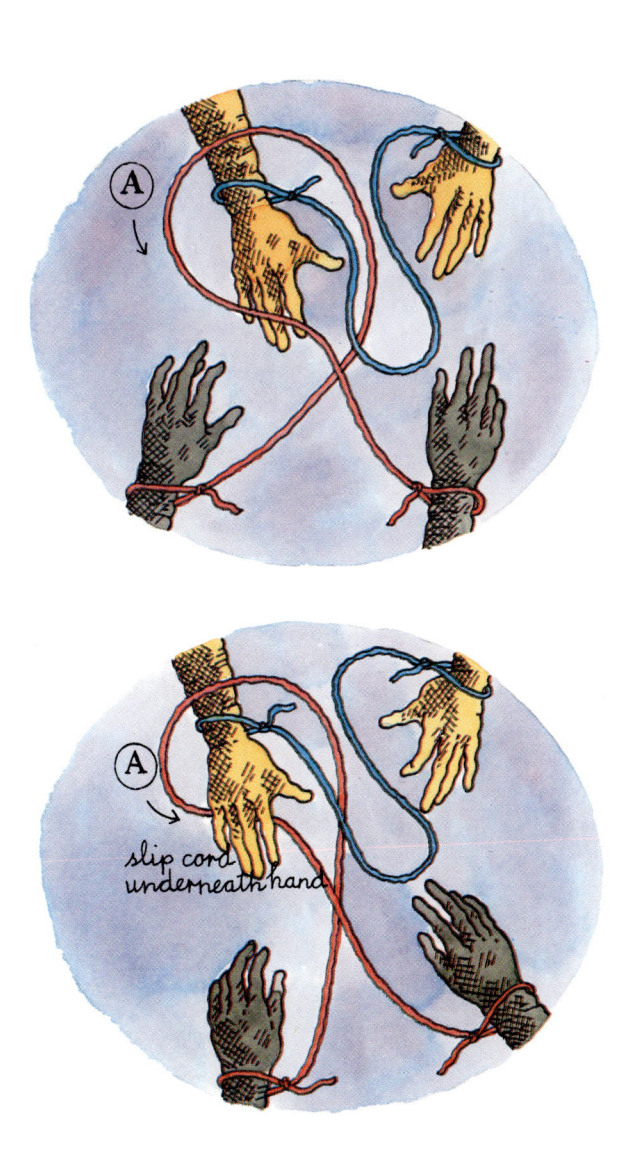

# Tangle Torture

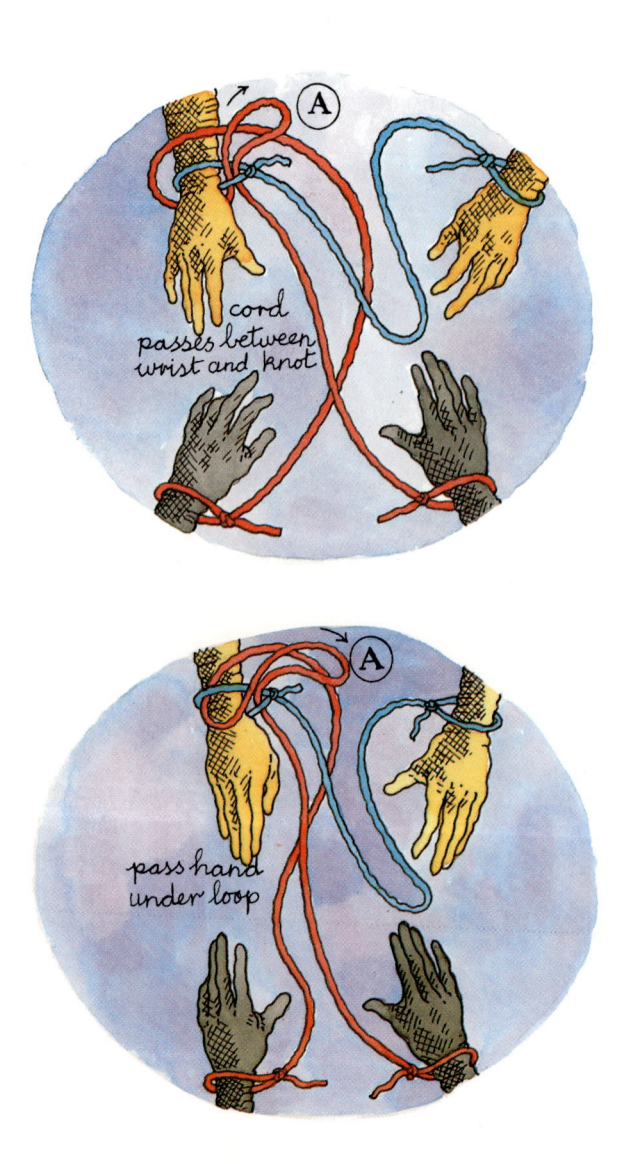

31

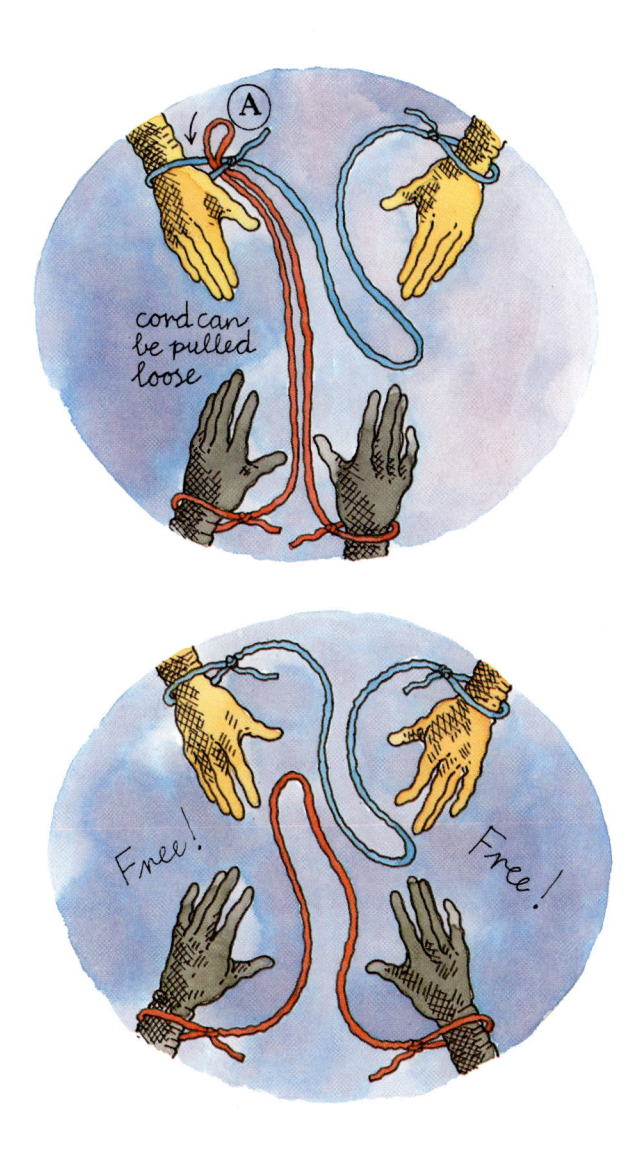

# STRONG PEOPLE DEFEATED
**Immobilize a Bossy Person**

Tell the bossiest person in the room that you are going to mesmerize him and take away all his powers. Get him to stand upright against a wall with both heels touching the base of the wall.

Drop some money on the floor about six inches in front of him and challenge him to pick up the money without moving his heels from the wall.
He will find it impossible and will probably fall over.

## Stuck to the Floor

Get someone to lie on his or her back full length on the floor with folded arms, and ankles tied together with a scarf or tie. Now tell this unfortunate person to get up without uncrossing his arms.

It's very tricky!

## Five Bricks with One Hand

Ask your friends to see how many bricks they can lift with one hand and then amaze them by picking up five at once.

*not like this*

*or this*

You can do this easily by stacking the bricks in a special way and lifting all five by picking up the bottom one.

*grasp brick at bottom of pile & LIFT*

*how is it possible?*

*don't ask me*

# SECRET MESSAGES
## Telepathic Tips

Convince everyone that you have telepathic powers by discovering which playing cards are held up in front of you, even though you have been blindfolded.

Before you display your powers you will need to have decided on a code with an assistant who must pretend to be an ordinary member of the audience in the front row, and send you secret signals.

Make sure that although you really are blindfolded you *can* look downwards and glimpse the hands and feet of your assistant.

As someone holds up a card and you appear to agonise over its identity, your friend can signal discreetly with hands and feet.

*ready to shuffle*

Card values from ace to ten can be shown by the fingers and thumbs of both hands.

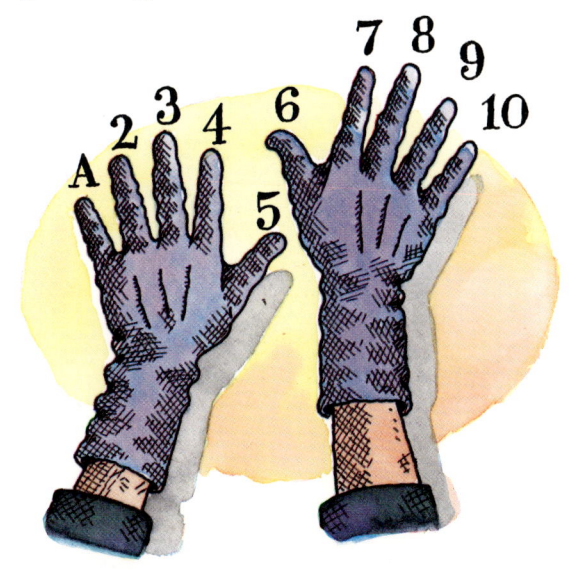

The left hand shows Ace to five, and the right hand shows six to ten.

Your friend can indicate the number by casually laying two fingers of the other hand over the appropriate finger or thumb.

Show the card suits by foot positions.

Both feet forward means hearts.

Left foot forward means spades.

Right foot forward means clubs. ♣

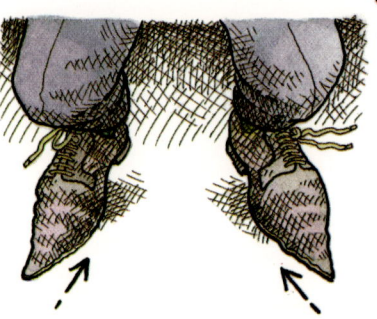

Both feet back means diamonds. ♦

Close the right hand for a Jack, the left for a Queen and both hands for a King. You can obviously vary the code by leg-twitching or foot-shuffling etc.

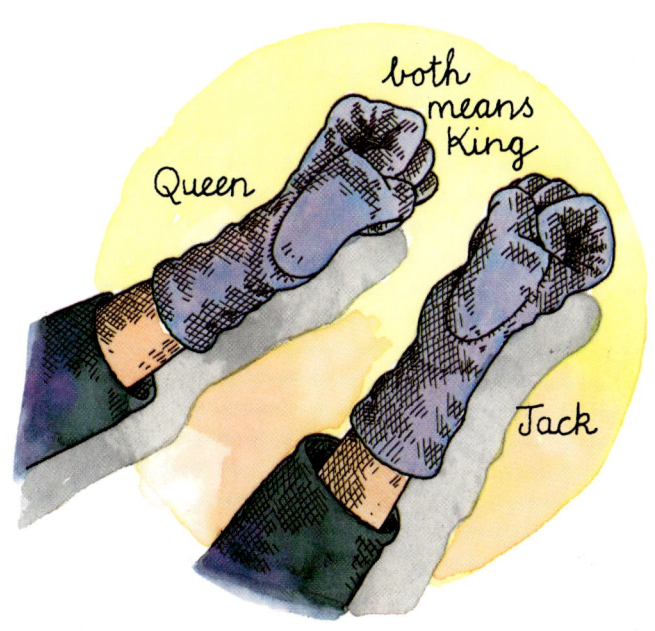

The audience will be amazed by your wonderful powers.

## Blank Pages

If you have something very private to tell a friend, send a message using invisible ink made from simple ingredients. Your secret will be revealed when the paper is heated gently, preferably near a light bulb.

You can use inks made from milk (the less creamy the better) or a teaspoon of sugar dissolved in a glass of water, or vinegar or lemon juice. Onion juice is good for really sad letters!

# FUN IN THE DARK

Amuse your friends or give them a fright by making shadow pictures.

You should do this in the dark but with a light source to make shadows on the wall.

Light sources such as moonlight, lightning, a flickering candelabra or a small spotlight are very effective.

On the next pages are some suggested shapes; you can invent others yourself.

# Gruesome Duck

# Giant Spider

Furry gloves and trembling hands are ideal for a convincing giant spider.

# Baying Dog

## Flapping Thing

## Unexpected Goose

# Lurking Stranger